MR. LAZY

by Roger Hargreaves

WORLD INTERNATIONAL

Mr Lazy lives in Sleepyland, which is a very lazylooking and sleepylike place.

The birds in Sleepyland fly so slowly they sometimes fall out of the sky.

The grass takes so long to grow it only needs cutting once a year.

Even the trees are lazylooking and sleepylike.

And do you know what time everybody gets up in Sleepyland?

The answer is, they don't get up in the morning.

They get up in the afternoon!

And, incidentally, this is what a Sleepyland clock looks like.

Everything takes so long to do there's only time for four hours a day!

Anyway, this story starts with Mr Lazy being fast asleep in bed. In Sleepyland they call that being slow asleep!

He spends rather a lot of time in bed. It's his favourite place to be!

He opened his eyes, yawned, yawned again – and went back to sleep.

Later, Mr Lazy opened his eyes again, yawned, yawned again, and went back to sleep again.

Much later, Mr Lazy got up and went to make his breakfast.

We say breakfast, although really it was teatime.

He put the kettle on to make some tea. Kettles take two hours to boil in Sleepyland!

Then he toasted a slice of bread. Bread takes three hours to go brown in Sleepyland.

Toast never gets burnt there!

While he was waiting for his kettle to boil and his bread to toast, Mr Lazy went into the garden of Yawn Cottage – which was where he lived.

He sat down on a chair. And you can probably guess what happened next.

That's right. He yawned, and yawned again, and went to sleep.

Suddenly he woke up with a jump, which is something that doesn't happen very often to Mr Lazy.

And the reason he woke up with a jump was because of the noise.

"WAKE UP," said the noise.

"WAKEUPWAKEUPWAKEUP."

There were two men standing in front of him.

"I'm Mr Busy," said one of the men.

"And I'm Mr Bustle," said the other.

"Come along now," said Mr Bustle busily.

"We can't have you sleeping all day," added Mr Busy, bustling Mr Lazy to his feet.

"But who are you?" asked Mr Lazy.

"We're Bustle and Busy," they replied.

"Oh," said Mr Lazy.

"Come along now," said Mr Busy, "we haven't got all day."

"But . . .," said Mr Lazy.

"No time for buts," said Mr Busy. "Or ifs," added Mr Bustle.

"There's the wood to chop and the beds to make and the floors to clean and the coal to get and the windows to polish and the plates to wash and the furniture to dust and the grass to cut and the hedges to clip and the food to cook!"

"And the clothes to mend," added Mr Busy.

"Oh dear," groaned Mr Lazy in a daze. "The wood to clean and the beds to get and the floors to cut and the coal to cook and the windows to make and the plates to mend and the furniture to chop and the grass to wash and the hedges to dust and the clothes to clip?"

He'd got it all completely wrong he was in such a daze.

Then Bustle and Busy set Mr Lazy to work.

Chopping and making and cleaning and getting and polishing and washing and dusting and cutting and clipping and cooking and mending.

Not to mention all the fetching and carrying!

Poor Mr Lazy!

"Now," they said when he'd finished, "it's time for a walk!"

And off they set on the longest walk Mr Lazy had ever been on.

Mr Lazy is one of those people who never walks when he has a chance of sitting down, and never sits down when he has a chance of lying down.

But this day he had no choice. They made him walk for miles and miles and miles, until he felt his legs must be worn right down to his body.

Poor Mr Lazy!

When they arrived back at Yawn Cottage, Mr Busy said, "Right! Now for a run!"

"Oh no," groaned Mr Lazy.

"When I blow this whistle," said Mr Bustle producing a whistle, "you've got to start running."

"As fast as you can," added Busy.

Mr Lazy groaned a deep groan, and closed his eyes.

Mr Bustle put the whistle to his lips.

"Wheeeeeeeeeeeeee," whistled the whistle.

"Wheeeeeeeeeeeeeeeeeee," went the whistle.

Mr Lazy, poor Mr Lazy, started to run.

But his legs weren't getting him anywhere.

He opened his eyes and looked down to see why.

And the reason his legs weren't getting him anywhere, was because he was sitting on a chair in the garden.

And there was no sign of Mr Busy and Mr Bustle!

It had all been a terrible dream!

And the whistle was the whistling kettle boiling in the kitchen!

Mr Lazy heaved a sigh of relief.

And then he went into the kitchen, and sat down to have his breakfast, and to think about his dream.

But you know what happened next, don't you?

"Wake up, Mr Lazy!"

"WAKEUPWAKEUPWAKEUP!"

3 Great Offers For Mr Men Fans

1 Token
EGMONT WORLD

1 FREE Door Hangers and Posters

In every Mr Men and Little Miss Book like this one you will find a special token. Collect 6 and we will send you either a brilliant Mr. Men or Little Miss poster and a Mr Men or Little Miss double sided, full colour, bedroom door hanger. Apply using the coupon overleaf, enclosing six tokens and a 50p coin for your choice of two items.

Egmont World tokens can be used towards any other Egmont World / World International token scheme promotions, in early learning and story / activity books.

Posters: Tick your preferred choice of either Mr Men ☐ or Little Miss ☐

Door Hangers: Choose from: Mr. Nosey & Mr Muddle ☐, Mr Greedy & Mr Lazy ☐, Mr Tickle & Mr Grumpy ☐, Mr Slow & Mr Busy ☐, Mr Messy & Mr Quiet ☐, Mr Perfect & Mr Forgetful ☐, Little Miss Fun & Little Miss Late ☐, Little Miss Helpful & Little Miss Tidy ☐, Little Miss Busy & Little Miss Brainy ☐, Little Miss Star & Little Miss Fun ☐. (Please tick)

ENTRANCE FEE
3 SAUSAGES

MR. GREEDY

2 Mr Men Library Boxes

Keep your growing collection of Mr Men and Little Miss books in these superb library boxes. With an integral carrying handle and stay-closed fastener, these full colour, plastic boxes are fantastic. They are just £5.49 each including postage. Order overleaf.

3 Join The Club

To join the fantastic Mr Men & Little Miss Club, check out the page overleaf NOW!

MR MEN and LITTLE MISS™ & © 1998 Mrs. Roger Hargreaves

Join Our Club!

MR. MEN & Little Miss CLUB

When you become a member of the fantastic Mr Men and Little Miss Club you'll receive a personal letter from Mr Happy and Little Miss Giggles, a club badge with your name, and a superb Welcome Pack (pictured below right).

You'll also get birthday and Christmas cards from the Mr Men and Little Misses, 2 newsletters crammed with special offers, privileges and news, and a copy of the 12 page Mr Men catalogue which includes great party ideas.

If it were on sale in the shops, the Welcome Pack alone might cost around £13. But a year's membership is just £9.99 (plus 73p postage) with a 14 day money-back guarantee if you are not delighted!

HOW TO APPLY To apply for any of these three great offers, ask an adult to complete the coupon below and send it with appropriate payment and tokens (where required) to: Mr Men Offers, PO Box 7, Manchester M19 2HD. Credit card orders for Club membership ONLY by telephone, please call: 01403 242727.

To be completed by an adult

❏ **1.** Please send a poster and door hanger as selected overleaf. I enclose six tokens and a 50p coin for post (coin not required if you are also taking up 2. or 3. below).

❏ **2.** Please send __ Mr Men Library case(s) and __ Little Miss Library case(s) at £5.49 each.

❏ **3.** Please enrol the following in the Mr Men & Little Miss Club at £10.72 (inc postage)

Fan's Name:_____Fan's Address:_____

_____Post Code:_____Date of birth:___/___/___

Your Name:_____Your Address:_____

Post Code:_____Name of parent or guardian (if not you):_____

Total amount due: £_____ (£5.49 per Library Case, £10.72 per Club membership)

❏ I enclose a cheque or postal order payable to Egmont World Limited.

❏ Please charge my MasterCard / Visa account.

Card number: | | | | | | | | | | | | | | | | |

Expiry Date: _____/_____   Signature: _____

Data Protection Act: If you do **not** wish to receive other family offers from us or companies we recommend, please tick this box ❏. Offer applies to UK only